T5-CVC-313

HELPING HANDS

WILDLIFE REHABILITATION AT WORK

BY J. P. MARSH

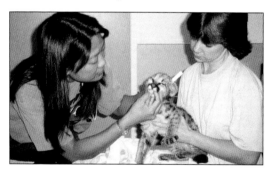

Celebration Press
Pearson Learning Group

CONTENTS

WILDLIFE AT RISK

Predators stalk them. Highways with speeding vehicles cut through their territory. Power lines crisscross their flyways. Bad weather threatens their food supply. Life for wild animals can be dangerous, whether from contact with humans or other hazards.

On a lonely stretch of road in northwest New Jersey, a van driver and her companion drive up a small hill. At the top a figure stands on the roadside. The van driver pulls over. The man beside the road points toward a huddled, shivering whitetail doe lying in the weeds. Could the nearby Woodlands Wildlife Refuge help?

A young black bear cub clings to a tree.

At a PAWS clinic just north of Seattle, a *veterinarian* examines a litter of rabbits for injuries and to determine their general health. A young camper found them under some bushes and brought them in. The vet knows the mother rabbit most likely left her little ones alone temporarily and did not abandon them as the camper feared. Now it will be almost impossible to return the rabbits to the nest.

While exploring near their home in Minnesota, a couple see a two-foot-tall bird standing next to an oak tree. Being bird watchers, they know it is a great horned owl. Even from 25 feet away, they can see that the magnificent bird is in trouble. There are feathers lying on the ground, and the owl is swaying back and forth. What can they do to help—call the Raptor Center?

A great horned owl

Situations like these happen every day. Luckily help is often nearby. People who find wildlife in distress can turn to wildlife rehabilitation workers. These experts know what to do for animals that have suffered misfortune and need aid.

Wildlife rehabilitation, or rehab, involves caring for sick, injured, or orphaned wild animals and restoring them to good health. The goal is to return the animals to their natural habitat.

Wildlife rehab is a job that requires special study and training. Rehab workers have to like animals, but sympathy for animals is not always enough. Knowing when *not* to help an animal is important, too. Often rehab workers must make hard decisions based on the animals' needs.

Wildlife rehabilitation is a labor of love for thousands of people across the country. Let's take a look at some of the challenges they face and the good work they do at three rehabilitation centers.

Wildlife rehabilitation workers are licensed by the U.S. Fish and Wildlife Service and the state in which they work. You must have a license to keep wild animals.

PAWS EXTENDS
A HELPING HAND

In Lynnwood, Washington, just north of Seattle, the Progressive Animal Welfare Society, or PAWS, manages the rehabilitation of wildlife in the region. Eagles, owls, ducks, songbirds, deer, bears, raccoons, and even flying squirrels have all gotten a helping hand there.

PAWS has another location in McCleary, Washington, near Olympia. Together the centers see and treat about 200 different species of animals!

Flying squirrels are among the many kinds of animals that have been helped by PAWS.

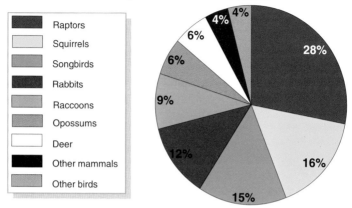

A staff of about 20 employees and 400 volunteers provide medical care and shelter at the PAWS centers. They have a difficult job. A medical doctor has only one species to treat—humans. A veterinarian, or vet, must help many different kinds of animals. Each animal species has specific problems and needs.

For a sick or injured animal, a trip to the PAWS clinic can be very frightening. The creature may be in pain or in shock. At PAWS, quiet surroundings and dim lighting help calm the animal.

A vet examines every animal to check its condition and then treats it for any illness or injury. The center also shelters and cares for each animal as it recovers or grows old enough to be released.

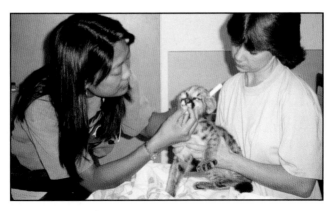

Workers at PAWS examine a baby bobcat.

Looking a wild animal in the eyes is predator behavior. To keep animals calm, wildlife workers try to avoid eye contact with their subjects whenever possible.

The shelters at PAWS are made for individual animals. Each species requires a specific environment to stay healthy. Size, temperature, and amount of light must all be just right. Living space for a 200-pound elk will naturally be quite different from that for a coyote or a porcupine.

The correct food is essential, too. Some animals will eat only live food. Young animals often need feeding around the clock. That means PAWS staff must be available 24 hours a day, every day of the year.

Providing medical care, shelter, and food is only part of the process for successful recovery. Three important factors make the work at PAWS and at any rehab facility harder: taming, habituation, and imprinting.

Sometimes people find wild animal babies, tame them, and keep them as pets. When these animals grow too large or hard to handle, the owners often bring them to PAWS. The outcome of this situation is generally difficult for everyone. A tame animal often can no longer survive in the wild. Nor can it be kept at a rehab facility forever either. There's not enough space or money to keep so many animals.

Problems can also arise if animals become habituated, or comfortable, with people and other animals while at the center. PAWS workers guard against this by keeping predators and prey totally separated. A rabbit must not get used to seeing a fox close by, or its life back in the wild would probably be short. For this reason PAWS also keeps contacts between wildlife and humans to a minimum.

Imprinting happens with baby animals. Some, especially birds, quickly learn to view any other animal nearby as their mother. It's easy to see how this could cause problems. Baby animals need to be with others of their own kind to grow up healthy.

Many baby songbirds need food about every 20 minutes, morning to evening. Baby mammals need feeding every few hours, 24 hours a day.

If all this sounds complicated, that's because it is. Rehabilitation takes time and money. Kip Parker is the director of the PAWS Wildlife Center. Parker has worked with animals for more than 30 years. For him the best part of rehabilitation work is setting a wild animal free. "Caring for these creatures is a complex affair. After weeks or months of concern, a bond is formed. It is uplifting to see them released and back on their own."

This raccoon has found a meal in a surburban garbage can.

In addition to his work at the center, Parker also lectures and writes about wildlife rehabilitation. Like most rehab facilities, PAWS depends on donations from the public to stay in business, and several PAWS staff members work full–time fundraising for animal care.

Many of us seldom have a chance to see an elk or a bear or even a coyote in the wild. Why should we care about rehab for animals we rarely see? Kip Parker would say, "Because the rewards are enormous! Rehabilitation is about the wonder and excitement of wild things. In helping wild animals and seeking knowledge about their lives, we gain insight into the world in which we live and our own place in it."

If you live in a big city and think wild animals have nothing to do with you, Parker has news for you. "There are whole, hidden populations of wildlife in a large city," he explains. "In fact, the density of wild animals in town can be much greater than that in the wilderness. Migrating birds fly through in thousands. Falcons and geese sometimes live there year-round. Raccoons and opossums find urban areas an excellent place, where food abounds. Wild animals are not intruders here," Parker insists. "We are in *their* backyard!"

RESCUES AT WOODLANDS WILDLIFE REFUGE

On the other side of the United States, in Clinton, New Jersey, Woodlands Wildlife Refuge has goals similar to those of PAWS. It is a nonprofit center for healing sick and injured wild animals, such as the whitetail doe mentioned on page 3, and returning them to their homes in the wild.

Woodlands faces the same challenges and uses many of the same methods as PAWS and other rehabilitation centers. The staff members, well trained in animal care, work with a local animal hospital.

Orphaned animals like the fawn seen here are given expert care at the Woodlands Wildlife Refuge.

Under the guidance of its tireless director, Tracy Nash, the Woodlands Wildlife Refuge enjoys strong support in the community. A number of dedicated volunteers give of their time and expert training in animal care.

Woodlands depends entirely on donations of money and needed items and equipment. Many local people are sponsors of the refuge and give monthly or yearly. Businesses and corporations also donate money and equipment.

Especially in the warm months, Woodlands is extremely busy with a wide variety of animals. From chipmunks to 500-pound black bears, common gray squirrels to red foxes, bats to box turtles, the center looks after animals of all sizes and shapes.

Woodlands treats injured animals and also performs orphan rescues. One orphaned animal that the refuge cared for was a black bear cub found by the New Jersey Division of Fish and Wildlife. This government agency protects and manages New Jersey's fish and wildlife.

Like its counterparts in other states, the New Jersey Division of Fish and Wildlife does "bear counts" in the winter months when bears are dormant, or inactive. They weigh the bears, if possible, check their health, and tattoo or tag them.

Sometimes the wildlife division employees also attach a radio collar to a bear to trace its movements. In doing so, they are able to learn a great deal about the local bear population, such as how many cubs females have and how long bears live.

Unfortunately, in this case, the bear they hoped to examine in midwinter wasn't as dormant as they had expected. She bolted from her den before they could give her a shot to make her unconscious.

She left behind a small cub, born just a few weeks earlier. The wildlife officers hoped the mother bear would return to the cub, but she didn't. The officers then placed the cub with another family of bears, thinking that the new mother might treat the little bear as her own. Again, this turned out to be wishful thinking.

In May the cub was spotted wandering in the woods, alone and at risk. In June, officers were able to capture him and took the feisty, snarling creature to Woodlands Wildlife Refuge.

At Woodlands they named the cub "the Brat" for his continued untamed behavior. Feeding him and cleaning his cage were exciting experiences. Attacks on the cage door were frequent and loud. Though the Brat was only a 25-pound baby, he could still terrify people.

Woodlands Wildlife Refuge has cared for and returned to the wild small black bear cubs like this one.

Nevertheless, the Woodlands workers were really quite pleased. The young bear was eating well, he was active, and above all he was acting as a wild bear should. They were confident that when released into the woods, the Brat would survive.

Seeing the bear eating blackberries one day, a young visitor suggested the name "Blackberry," (or Black-bear-y)! After all, "the Brat" is hardly an agreeable name. Everyone liked the new name much better, and from then on "Blackberry" it was.

Blackberry grew quickly and became stronger. By mid-September it was clear to the Woodlands staff that the time had come to return him to the wild.

They planned for the big day. Together with New Jersey Fish and Wildlife workers, they would first sedate Blackberry, or give him a drug to make him unconscious. They would weigh him, take some important measurements, and tag one ear with an identification number.

Sedating a wild animal can be very tricky. The medicines used are dangerous, and if too much is given, the results can be deadly. The wildlife workers thought Woodlands' bear orphan weighed about 80 pounds, so they used the amount of medicine for an 80-pound bear.

Surprise! Blackberry actually weighed 120 pounds, and after getting his shot, he was a sleepy but very unhappy bear. The workers managed to adjust his dosage of medicine, however, and the rest of the work of checking his heart and breathing and tagging him went smoothly.

It was October and in the woods of northwestern New Jersey the leaves were at their peak of color. The brisk air smelled clean. It was a fine day to be a bear! In a cage on the back of a truck stood a wild bear breathing the scent of home.

A young black bear roams freely in the wild.

The cage was opened, and everyone stepped back and watched. Blackberry looked out, climbed down from the truck, and nosed around for a bit. After a few false starts and some exploration, he probably understood that all that space was his for the taking.

Blackberry took off for the deeper forest at top speed. No long goodbyes—he just headed into the woods, apparently enjoying his freedom. That was just the thank-you the folks of Woodlands Wildlife Refuge were hoping for.

SOARING WINGS AT THE RAPTOR CENTER

On the grounds of the St. Paul campus of the University of Minnesota is another rehabilitation center, this one devoted to birds of prey, which hunt animals or eat dead animals. Called raptors, these birds include owls, hawks, eagles, falcons, and vultures.

Enter The Raptor Center and you will see glass walls and huge skylights that let in the bright sunshine. It takes little imagination to see the building as a huge aerie (AY ur ee), or mountain nest for birds.

The bald eagle Leuc, who is 22 years old, is the senior education eagle at The Raptor Center.

Near the entrance are two bald eagles, looking proud on their perch in a glass enclosure. Their enclosure is attached to the side of the building on a hillside. From their perch they have the view they might command if they were free.

Unfortunately, some of the birds at The Raptor Center will never be free. One bald eagle, named Leuc, has been at The Raptor Center since 1983. He was found on the highway with a badly dislocated right shoulder. Although treated, he can't extend his wing well enough to fly.

There is always a flow of activity at The Raptor Center, a constant traffic of birds from outside to inside. It seems as if each staff member has a raptor perched on his or her fist. Heavy leather gloves protect them from the birds' sharp talons.

One of the staff offers a tidbit of fish to a young bald eagle. This bird may be young, but he's two feet tall and his beak looks as if it could tear through anything. Another staff member carries a great horned owl wth eyes like twin suns.

The eyes of owls are made to take in enormous amounts of light. Their eyes are fixed and can't be moved from side to side. Owls must turn their heads to look around.

Most Common Injuries or Conditions Seen by U.S. Rehabilitation Centers

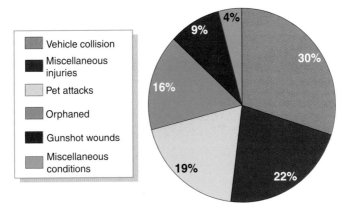

Founded in 1972, The Raptor Center receives injured birds from around the world, such as the great horned owl mentioned on page 4. Injuries to raptors are increasing. Collisions with power lines and trucks, poisonings, and illegal hunting result in a constant flow of new patients.

The center works with the University of Minnesota, known for its expertise in animal medicine. The dedicated staff and volunteers can help many of the birds brought there.

Any raptor that does not heal well enough to fly perfectly cannot be released, however. If it is otherwise healthy, the bird becomes a living teaching tool, a means of increasing our knowledge about these amazing animals.

Humans have had a long association with birds of prey. Years ago people developed a way of restoring broken or missing flight feathers of birds they used in hunting. The Raptor Center still uses the process, called imping, which involves placing the shafts of new feathers onto old ones, if about an inch of shaft remains. Since the shaft of a feather is hollow, the repair is fairly simple.

First a new feather is found to replace the old one. Selecting the correct feather is an important step. It must be from the same kind of bird, on the correct side, and of the same size as the old feather.

Next, the new feather is trimmed to be the right length when joined to the shaft of the old one. Then a dowel—a round rod—of bamboo is glued inside the new shaft, and both are joined to the old shaft with glue. A vet sedates the raptor if a lot of feathers are replaced. These replacements are temporary, allowing flight until the bird grows new feathers after molting.

After a raptor has recovered, it must regain its fitness through feeding and exercise. Then it can fly free again. Twice a year The Raptor Center schedules special release days. On these days the center returns successfully rehabilitated raptors to the wild.

About 45 percent of raptors treated at The Raptor Center are successfully returned to the wild.

Imagine attending one of these events! Maybe you have been chosen to give one of these splendid animals back to the sky. You put on a special glove and hold this blindfolded wild creature on your hand. Then you remove the blindfold, count to three, and toss the bird up into the air.

People are clapping and cheering. Do you feel as though you are up there soaring with the raptor? You just gave a wild animal back its freedom. This is what wildlife rehabilitation is all about!

WHAT SHOULD YOU DO?

Commonsense Tips for Wild Animal Rescue

If you find an injured or orphaned animal, centers like the ones discussed in this book have some advice for you.

• Before you take any action, observe and collect as much information as you can. Although a baby animal may look abandoned, it may not be. The mother may have left the youngster alone for just a short time. Animals sometimes have to travel some distance for food. Mothers try to leave their babies in a safe place.

• If an animal looks sick or injured, call a wildlife professional or veterinarian and tell him or her everything you have seen. That person will offer you the proper advice or help at this point.

• Do NOT approach or touch an injured or sick animal. Animals that seem calm, such as deer, can deliver a kick that might cause great harm. Sick animals may also harbor zoonoses (zoh AHN uh seez), diseases that humans can get from animals. Rabies, a fatal disease, can be passed from animals to people, as can other diseases, such as tularemia (rabbit fever).

• DO call for help—you might save an animal's life or help one in great pain!

GLOSSARY

aerie nesting place of birds on a cliff or mountain

dormant inactive or sleeping

flight feather large feather in the wing or tail of a bird that is needed for the bird to fly

habitat place where an animal or plant naturally lives or grows

habituation getting used to something, as when wild animals get used to being around people

imping process used to replace broken flight feathers with sound ones

imprinting process in which a newborn animal learns to recognize a nearby animal or person as its mother

molting periodic shedding of feathers before new ones grow in

predator animal that lives by catching and eating other animals

raptor bird of prey. Examples include owls, hawks, eagles, falcons, and vultures.

rehab short for rehabilitation, the process of helping to restore an animal to good health

species grouping of plants or animals that are thought to be very closely related

talon claw of a bird of prey

taming causing an animal to lose behaviors that help it succeed as a wild animal

veterinarian person trained and usually licensed to treat injuries and diseases of animals

zoonoses diseases that humans can catch from animals